D1826182

CLICK
CLICK
CLICK
CLICK
CLICK
CLICK
CLICK
UNIVERSITY OF WATERLOO
HELLO DR. GATTI.
KNOCK KNOCK
OH JEN! SORRY I LOST TRACK OF THE TIME.
PLEASE, HAVE A SEAT.

SO MISS CHOI YOUR MASTERS WORK IN QUANTUM COMPUTING IS ASTOUNDING.
I AM THOROGHLY IMPRESSED.
WHERE DO YOU SEE YOUR PHD RESEARCH GOING FROM HERE?
WELL... MY RESEARCH IN QUANTUM COMPUTING CAN FURTHER THE ABILITIES OF PRECOGNITIVE VISIONS THROUGH POSSIBILITY MAPPING.
WHAT!?
AND I HYPOTHESIZE MY RESEARCH CAN HELP FURTHER YOUR WORK IN QUANTUM BRANCHING.
HOW SO?
WELL ...

WELL MY COMPUTATIONAL WORK WILL BE ABLE TO PREDICT A NUMBER OF SCENARIOS THAT ARE POSSIBILITIES.
FROM THOSE POSSIBILITIES WE CAN DERIVE WHICH ONES ARE SEEN BY PRECOGNITIVES.
YOUR PHD THESIS ON ALTERNATE PROBABILITIES WAS WHAT MOTIVATED ME TO START WORKING WITH QUANTUM COMPUTING.
I WANT QUANTUM COMPUTING TO BE USED FOR PRACTICAL APPLICATIONS
IMAGINE BEING ABLE TO CHOOSE THE FUTURE INSTEAD OF MITIGATING IT.

WELL... I HAVE TO RUN THE APPLICATION THROUGH THE BOARD...
BUT YOU HAVE MY APPROVAL.
I'M RELIEVED TO HEAR THAT

SUDBURY
CHEAP
CHIRP
CHIRP
CHEAP
YOU'LL REALLY LIKE HIM. HE'S REALLY NICE.
HERE'S HIS HOUSE!
WHO ARE YOU WAVING TO?
OH FUNNY BIL! DON'T WORRY TOMMY, BILLS JUST PULLING OUR LEGS!
UGHHHHHHH
I DIDN'T KNOW YOU WERE SO FUNNY.

SHE MUST BE JOKING.
OF COURSE!
WINK
I'M NOT JOKING AROUND!
MISS DUPONT AND MISS NIEMENEN WHAT SEEMS TO BE THE MATTER?
OH IT'S NOTHING. SYBIL IS JUST TRYING TO PULL A PRANK ON MY FRIEND TOMMY.
TOMMY?

YEAH HE'S RIGHT HERE!
HONEY... TOMMY MORTIMER WAS HIT BY A CAR AND DIED TEN YEARS AGO.
BEFORE YOU WERE BORN.
WHAT?
UNLESS
I'LL CALL YOUR PARENTS MISS NIEMENSEN.

IT SEEMS YOU ARE GIFTED.

THE NEXT MORNING
SO WE WON'T BE IN SCHOOL TOGETHER NEXT YEAR...
WHAT DO YOU MEAN?

MY PARENTS SAY I'M SPECIAL...
I'M GIFTED... AND GIFTED CHILDREN GO TO A DIFFERENT SCHOOL
OH...
I ALWAYS KNEW YOU WE'RE A FREAK!
PHWIP

PEOPLE WITH ABILITIES ARE FREAKS Y'KNOW.
YOU'RE NOT LIKE ANYONE ELSE.
YOU CREEP THEM OUT.
SURE
PSHHH
Woooo...

HEY STOP THAT!
DON'T YOU HIT HIM OR I'LL TELL YOUR TEACHER!
YOU'LL GET DETENTION!
WOOOSH
A FREAK?
GIRLS SIT NEAR THE FRONT WHERE I CAN SEE YOU.
A FREAK
...

I THINK I'M LOST ....
IRIS'S?
ALL THE WAY OUT HERE?
WHAT!

I WAS IN THE FOREST A SECOND AGO ...
MY BODY FEELS WEIRD TOO ...
WHAT!?
IS THAT ME?
I'M SO OLD!
WHERE AM I!?
BANG!

WHAT WAS THAT!
IT CAME FROM THAT DIRECTION!
HEY BIL ...

WHAT BRINGS YOU HERE?

CAW
CAW-
WHAT JUST HAPPENED ...
SYBIL HELEN! THERE YOU ARE!
CRACK
CRUNCK
I WAS SO WORRIED.
YOU WANDERED OFF THE MAIN TRAIL.
WE NEED TO GO BACK AND TAKE THE OTHER TRAIL.

CRACK
CRACKLE
NOW BE CAREFUL,
I DON'T WANT YOU TO BURN YOUR HANDS
MY HANDS ...
THAT MAN ... HE WAS SHOT ... HE DIED ...
WHEN I TOUCHED THAT FLOWER
I DON'T WANT TO BE DIFFERENT
SYBIL, DEAR YOU'RE GETTING CLOSE !

SIZZLE
SYBIL WHAT ARE YOU DOING!?
I NEVER WANT TO SEE THAT AGAIN!

I'VE WAITED FOR THIS MOMENT FOR SO LONG....
FINALLY THE DAY HAS COME.

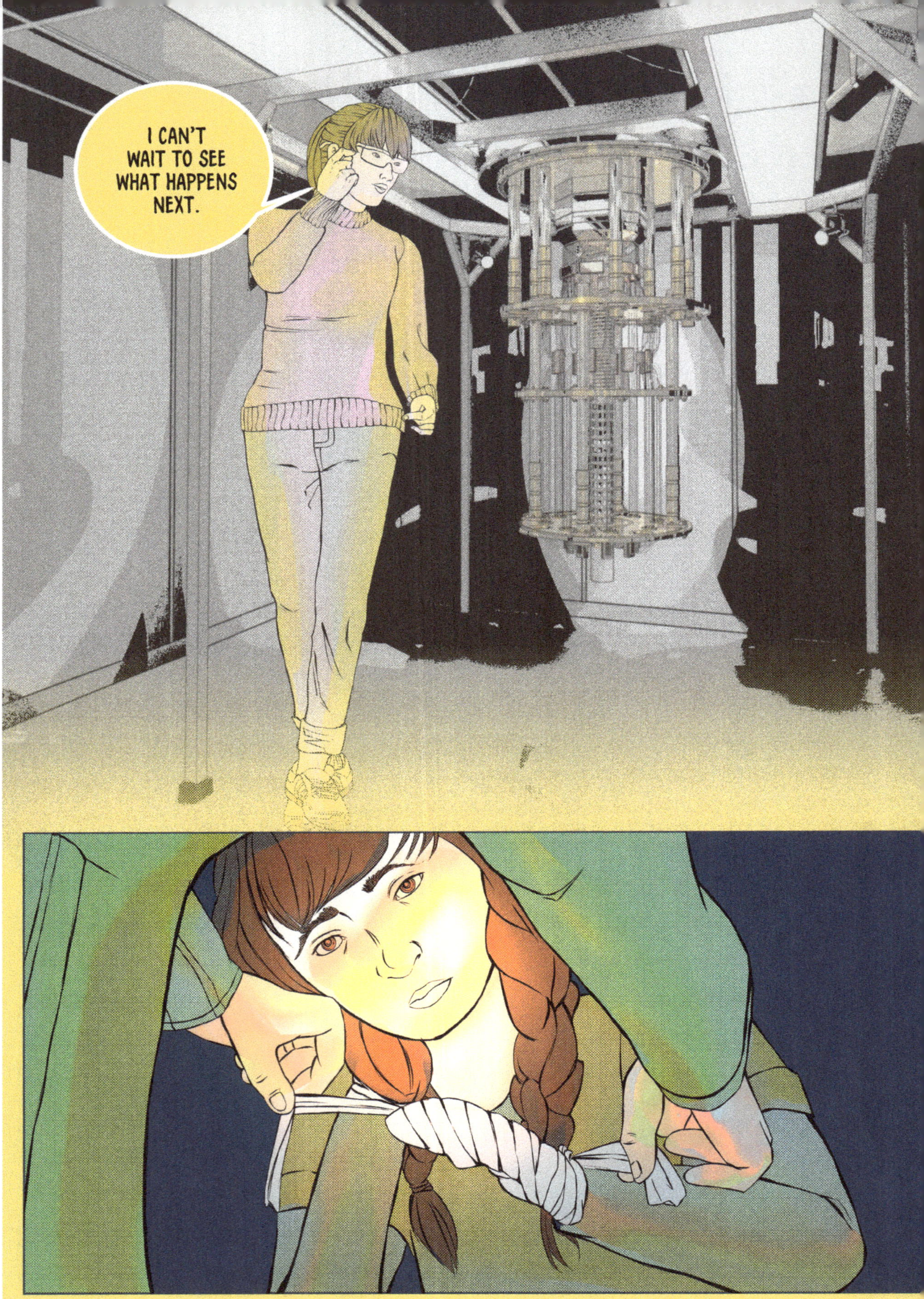
I CAN'T WAIT TO SEE WHAT HAPPENS NEXT.

CPSIA information can be obtained
at www.ICGtesting.com
Printed in the USA
LVHW071350120519
617539LV00018B/777/P

9 781989 481004